the Blue-Nosed Witch

by Margaret Embry

pictures by Carl Rose

A BANTAM SKYLARK BOOK®
TORONTO • NEW YORK • LONDON • SYDNEY • AUCKLAND

RL 3, 007-010

THE BLUE-NOSED WITCH

*A Bantam Book / published by arrangement with
Holiday House, Inc.*

PRINTING HISTORY

*Holiday House edition published September 1956
12 printings through August 1980*

*Bantam edition / June 1983
2nd printing . . . October 1984
3rd printing . . . October 1985
4th printing . . . January 1986
5th printing . . . October 1986*

ISBN 0-553-15435-4

Published simultaneously in the United States and Canada

*Bantam Books are published by Bantam Books, Inc. Its trademark,
consisting of the words "Bantam Books" and the portrayal of
a rooster, is Registered in U.S. Patent and Trademark Office
and in other countries. Marca Registrada. Bantam Books, Inc.,
666 Fifth Avenue, New York, New York 10103.*

PRINTED IN THE UNITED STATES OF AMERICA

CW   14   13   12   11   10   9   8

for *Merry,*
who
originally
owned
Brockett

Not more than four or five Halloweens ago there was a very young witch named Blanche who owned a broom, a black kitten called Brockett, and a bright blue nose. She belonged to a very special scurry of witches, Scurry No. 13, known in the best witch circles all over the country for its beautiful flight formation.

The Grand Madame, who had been leader of the club for as long as any of them could remember, flew center front. She used a vacuum cleaner instead of a broom, and when she gunned her motor it sounded as exciting as a fire siren.

On the far right was Minnie Max waving her blood-red finger nails in the dark; they really did shine like rubies. And on the far left was Blanche's best friend, Josephine, who had long yellow fluorescent teeth that gleamed like stars.

In between and a little behind flew the nine rather ordinary witches who were only expected to follow the Grand Madame's lead, and cackle with horrid glee at appropriate times.

And last came Blanche, usually far, far behind. If it hadn't been for her marvelous blue nose that she could turn on and off at will, she wouldn't have been allowed in Scurry No. 13 at all.

Blanche was always late. She had good intentions and a dependable alarm clock, but somehow she never could get started any place on time. Something always happened at the last minute to delay her. Brockett, the black kitten, would run away, or Blanche would have misplaced her broom, or she would have to finish her comic, or have just one more piece of bread and peanutbutter and honey.

"You see," said Minnie Max to Josephine, "Blanche is still just a baby, and she ought to be sent back to Scurry No. 2½. Then she'd have to ride a whisk broom, not go any higher than the tops of the poplar trees, and never stay out after midnight with the rest of the grownups. If she's late one more time, I'm going to report her to the Grand Madame!"

"I know Blanche is young and scatterbrained," agreed Josephine, "but don't bother the Grand Madame with it. I'll take care of her. I promise she'll be on time for our next flight meeting."

"That's Halloween night," Minnie Max warned. "Sharp at midnight we're tak-ing off from Dead

Man's Bluff. Afterwards, if we make a good showing against the moon, there'll be dancing and chanting and a pot of brew. You'd better see that Blanche is at least half an hour early."

"I'll have her there on time," promised Josephine, "if I have to set her alarm an hour ahead."

As it turned out, Josephine switched the clock ahead not one hour but two, just for good measure. That probably would have been all right, but Blanche herself, as she was getting ready for bed at noon the day of Halloween, had the same good idea. She wound her clock

and set it ahead an extra hour and a half—and then just a little more in case Brockett would be hard to find.

But when the alarm shrieked that evening, Brockett for once was perched demurely on the bedpost right where she belonged, her fur newly licked smooth. Blanche yawned and brushed the straw out of her hair and rolled out of bed without her usual dilly-dallying. She washed her face and hands and polished up her blue nose. Her broom

9

was standing neatly behind the kitchen door.

Brockett hopped on eagerly without having to be coaxed. The clock said quarter of twelve, midnight. Actually, of course, it was scarcely half-past eight when they padlocked the front door and poked the key under the mat.

"It's not very dark out," said Blanche to the kitten as they soared over town. "We're probably much, much too early. Wonder if anyone is there yet?"

Blanche looked down below and saw a strange procession marching along the sidewalk. She dived lower for a better view. There was quite a tall witch in the lead.

"Why, that looks like Josephine. But whatever is she doing with that crowd? And *walking*? Maybe her broom broke down."

There were three ghosts, a pirate, a cowboy car-

rying a six-shooter and a lighted pumpkin, and a gypsy with spangled earrings.

Blanche settled down on the sidewalk and fell in step beside the tall witch. At once she saw it wasn't Josephine.

"Oh, excuse me," said Blanche. "I thought you were somebody I know."

The tall witch turned and stared. She had a rubbery look to her face, and her hair was stringy and obviously false. Josephine was always so careful about her hair.

"Hey!" shouted one of the ghosts, "where did you get that blue light on your nose? That's really neat!"

The little pirate, pulling at Blanche's skirts, pleaded, "Lemme see it! Lemme see it!"

"How does it work?" asked the cowboy, setting down his pumpkin.

So Blanche showed them. She made her nose glow bright and then fade palely away, then bright again and wink off and on like a turn signal.

"Gee," said the cowboy, "that's swell. I didn't see anything like that over at the dime store. Where did you buy it?"

"Lemme try it! Lemme try it?" begged the pirate, pulling again.

"I didn't buy it," Blanche said primly, "and I can't take it off and let you try it. But I'll do it again for you if you'll quit yanking my dress."

"Leave her alone, Butch," said the tall witch, giving the pirate a shove. Turning to Blanche she explained, "He's my little brother. I told Mother he was too young to go out Halloweening with us, but he always has to tag along."

"Oh, that's all right," Blanche said generously. "I don't mind letting him see if he wants to." She leaned down so Butch could feel her nose carefully.

"Hey, if you show us how the switch works I'll give you one of my jelly doughnuts," the biggest ghost offered, holding out a brown paper bag.

Blanche grinned at them. "There really isn't a switch at all," she said. "It just works by concentration. I think about lighting up my nose and it begins to glow. When I want it to shine very bright, I think hard, like this." She wrinkled her forehead and squinted her eyes. The nose glowed

a bright clear blue. "See? Simply concentration."

The ghost opened his bag. "That's really super!" he said. "Here, have a doughnut."

Blanche reached in eagerly. She hadn't had a

 jelly doughnut in weeks and weeks. "Where did you get these? They're wonderful!" she said, chewing happily.

"Over at Smith's. They have the best stuff. Last year it was caramel apples. Come along and we'll show you which house."

Blanche trailed along willingly, with Butch the pirate holding firmly to her hand.

"What's your name?" he asked as they walked along.

"I'm Blanche," she said.

"Blanche who?" Butch's sister, the tall witch, asked.

"Just Blanche."

"She's Blanche Witch, that's who," Butch said reasonably.

The cowboy turned around mischievously. "Which witch?"

16

And all the ghosts joined in with great glee, "Blanche Witch, that's which witch!"

They climbed the steps to Smith's front porch, all chanting the refrain, "Blanche Witch, that's which witch!"

The gypsy rang the doorbell.

A man with white hair opened the door. He gaped. "But—"

"Candy or cake or your windows we'll break!" they yelled at him.

"But you kids have all been here before," he protested.

"Yes, but *she* hasn't!" they laughed, pushing Blanche in front of Mr. Smith.

"Her nose turns on and off," said the pirate. "Show him!"

Blanche showed him obligingly.

"Say, that's really something!" said the man. "Come here, Mother, and see this!"

A lady sitting in a rocking chair got up and came over to the door. She gave a little gasp when she saw Blanche's nose. "Whatever will they think of next! These modern kids!"

"Sure, that's worth two doughnuts at least," said Mr. Smith. "Hold your sack."

"She hasn't got one," said the pirate, who had noticed right away.

Mrs. Smith bustled right off to her kitchen and returned with a brown paper bag.

"There, now," she said. "And here are three jelly doughnuts, and I put in some nuts and candy corn too, because you might not have time to go to many more houses."

"Thank you, ma'am," said Blanche, remembering her manners. "And please, could you tell me what time it is?"

Her husband pulled out his pocket watch. "Let's

18

see, it's just six and a half minutes after nine
o'clock."

"Just after nine o'clock?" Blanche asked bewil-
dered. "But I thought it was nearly midnight. The
time seems to be all turned around."

"It usually is on Halloween," laughed Mr. Smith.
"Anything can happen tonight. Well, good night,
kids, and don't soap any windows!"

"We won't," they shouted, racing down the
steps. "Good night, and thanks!"

19

They stopped at the corner and looked at each other a little uncertainly, trying to decide just what to do next.

"Oh-h!" cried Blanche in a panic. "I've lost my broom and my cat!"

The tall witch stared at her. "Broom? You didn't have any broom with you."

"She did too," the pirate said, "with a little black kitty sitting on the sweep part."

"I'll bet she left it back on Maple Street where

we stopped to look at her nose," said the gypsy. "Let's all walk back and help her find her stuff."

The gypsy was right. The broom was exactly where Blanche had left it leaning against a tree.

Brockett was perched up in the branches spitting at a yellow dog who was circling around below. Brockett refused to come down until the cowboy shooed the dog away. Then she jumped lightly down onto her mistress's shoulder.

Blanche shifted the kitten to a more comfortable position, and looked around happily. "Well, what do we do now? There's plenty of time."

"I can go to only one more place," said the short ghost. "So let's hurry!"

"Yes, we promised Mom we'd have him back by nine-fifteen," said the biggest ghost.

"No, it was nine-thirty," said the middle-sized ghost.

"As long as we're out this far," the gypsy suggested, "why don't we circle back by way of Old Man Skinner's house? He has apples."

The others stared at the gypsy in alarm.

"He's mean," the pirate explained to Blanche.

"He sure is." The cowboy nodded in agreement, and set down his pumpkin. "Old Man Skinner said we stole his apples, and we didn't. The wind blew them down, but he wouldn't believe us."

"That was way last year," said the gypsy. "He's maybe changed his mind by now, and everybody says he's got the best apples in town. I'd sure like one now. Let's go." She started walking.

"Bet he hasn't changed," said the biggest ghost, holding back the other two ghosts. "He hit my dog with a rock last summer just because we were cutting across the back of his lot on our way down to the creek."

"Yeh, Old Man Skinner's got a sling-shot and he's a good shot with it too," said the middle-sized ghost. "I've seen him hit birds with it way up on telephone wires. He said they were eating his cherries."

"Oh that was last spring," said the gypsy airily. "Let's just go out and call on him."

"Maybe he's lonely," said Blanche. She was

thinking of those apples. "We can say 'Trick or treat' very politely, and maybe he'll treat for once."

The cowboy picked up his pumpkin.

"I'm game, Blanche," he said. "I'll go with you, but I can tell you right now he doesn't like kids, especially on Halloween."

"But he's never seen Blanche," the tall witch said. "Maybe if he saw her wonderful nose—"

"Yes," said the gypsy, "let's go out there and show him Blanche's keen blue nose. Then maybe

24

he'll give us some apples. He's got some special
good ones this year. I saw them on the trees."

They formed another procession. Blanche was
in the lead in this bunch. She carried her broom
over her shoulder, with Brockett sitting in place on
the end.

The road was long and twisty. Blanche was
limping a little before they got there. Her feet hurt
because she wasn't used to walking so far. But she
didn't let on.

25

There was a light behind the curtains of Mr. Skinner's house, and smoke coming out of his chimney.

They climbed onto the porch giggling nervously.

Miss Gypsy gave a brave one-two-three knock.

No answer.

"He must be home," whispered the tall witch. "He has a fire in his fireplace."

They waited, then all of them pounded noisily. At once the door opened a crack, and a thin long nose hanging over a tight little mustache poked out at them.

The cowboy raised his pumpkin, even though the candle was burned out by now. "Trick or treat?" he asked hopefully.

At this, the door opened wider. Two suspicious eyes glared.

"Halloweening, is it? You young pests go home

where you belong. I've no time for your nonsense."

"Please, sir," said Blanche sweetly, "may we have some apples?"

"Apples!" snorted the man. He scowled at Blanche a moment, then said, "Want some apples, heh? You wait right here."

As soon as he had disappeared, the gypsy and the tall witch nodded, as if to say didn't we tell you?

But the pirate said, "Maybe he didn't go to get apples. Maybe he went for his sling-shot."

"Shut up, Butch," his sister whispered. "He's gone down the cellar for apples."

The gypsy shook her earrings and straightened her scarf. She wasn't so sure now.

28

"I wanna go home," said the smallest ghost in a trembling voice.

"Yes," said the biggest ghost, shakily too, "we promised Mom we'd be home with him by nine-fifteen!"

At that moment Mr. Skinner returned holding a small cardboard box filled with some smallish apples.

"Thanks, gee, thanks!" everybody said surprised as he handed the apples around.

The apples looked red and good in the light

from the door. Everybody at about the same time bit into them.

"Igg-puh!" they all said, spitting out.

The apples were mushy and brown inside and tasted terrible.

"You came here yapping for apples, didn't you?" yapped Mr. Skinner. "And I gave you apples, didn't I? What's the matter, aren't they good enough for you? They were good enough last year when you came around and tried to steal them and broke all my tree limbs."

"No, we didn't, honest, Mr. Skinner," pleaded the biggest ghost.

30

"And who stole all my green corn, and frightened my hens so they wouldn't lay? And then you come around here begging for my good apples. Well, they're all picked and sold, so you can just go home or I'll—"

"Flash your nose at him!" whispered the pirate, tugging at Blanche's skirts. "Scare him!"

Blanche winked her nose on and off venomously, but he just snorted at her and slammed the door.

"Why, he wasn't even *impressed!*" said the gypsy in fury. "It's a perfectly frightening nose too!"

31

"Let's soap his windows," said the middle-sized ghost. "Anybody got any soap?"

"Too bad none of the kids carry it any more," sighed the tall witch. "It'd be good to have some in case of an emergency, like this."

"I know," Blanche whispered. "Brockett, you do something. Up on that windowsill with you, and give him the you-know-what."

The black cat's eyes got yellower. Softly she leaped up to the windowsill, then stretched up onto her hind legs, and scritch-scratched with her front claws up and down the screen. It sounded worse than gravel being grated on a sidewalk and squeaky chalk on a blackboard. On top of this she let out a caterwauling yowl that tore through the night, frightful enough to make people jump out of their shoes.

The door flew open and out rushed Mr. Skinner, madder than an old hornet. He had his slingshot, and he meant business!

Everybody turned at once and fled. He took after them down the road, but he was too angry to aim well. The stones from his slingshot spattered at their feet, but nobody was hit.

On her broom meanwhile, Blanche spiralled

around his house and up to the chimney. Smoke was curling out of it.

"He's got a mighty cozy fire down there," she said to herself, "but he won't have it for long."

She landed on the steep ridge of the roof and then climbed cautiously down to the big brick chimney. Leaning her broom against it, she boosted herself up, so she could blow down it.

Putting a hearth-fire out was a trick that Minnie Max had taught her only a week or so before, and this was Blanche's first chance to try it by herself.

She took a big breath of air and blew down the chimney as hard as she could, thinking just the right words as she did this and giving each blow just the right swirl. With the third blow-down, the smoke slunk back. She raised her head and took another deep gulp of fresh air and blew again. She blew again and again until her ears buzzed and her nose turned green.

34

Down below, the smoke came out of the opened door in a great cloud. Mr. Skinner, thinking for sure his house was on fire, stopped chasing his visitors, and ran back toward the porch.

Blanche straddled her broom and gave a spring up into the air. Down she swooped over his head, buzzing him and laughing, but he was running too fast to see her.

She caught up with the rest of the crowd on the corner of Maple Street, where they had gathered around Brockett. The gypsy was trembling so much her earrings were jingling like sleighbells. The short ghost had torn his sheet, and the eye holes in his pillowcase were switched way around to the back of his head so he couldn't see which way he was going.

"Gollee!" breathed the cowboy, as Blanche dismounted from her broom. "That sure beats walking!"

"Doesn't it have a switch either?" the tallest ghost asked.

Blanche smiled. "No, it doesn't need a switch."

"Not even an engine?" asked the middle ghost.

Blanche thought a minute. "Well, I guess there's a sort of one."

"What kind of fuel do you use?" the tallest ghost asked again.

"Well—" Blanche hesitated again.

The cowboy said, "It doesn't need fuel, dope. It works by concentration, like her nose."

"Yes, I guess that's it," said Blanche. "I think how high I need to fly, and that's all there is to it."

"Lemme try it!" the pirate begged. "I can con-some-trate!"

"No, you don't!" said his sister. "You'd fall off and break your arm just like you did on the tire swing."

38

"It only works for me," said Blanche.

"I've *got* to go home!" said the smallest ghost in a muffled tone, trying to pull his pillowcase straight.

"So have we," the tall witch said, grabbing at her little brother. "So long, Blanche!"

"Here, I want to give her these, first," said the pirate, wriggling out of her grasp. He dropped three sticky black jelly beans into Blanche's sack.

When she tried to thank him he shouted back, "Oh, that's all right. I only like the orange kind."

Blanche and Brockett soared over town again. The streets were nearly deserted and most of the houses were dark. "I can't understand why people always want to go to bed so early. Just when things are beginning to get interesting," Blanche said to Brockett. "If somebody were only still awake, we could ring some more doorbells."

A little farther on, she looked down and saw a lighted house with several cars parked along the street in front of it.

"Look, maybe it's a party, and they might have some extra candy and nuts."

She landed expertly on the front lawn and almost before she could ring the bell, the door was opened wide.

"Hello!" said a man. "Come on in—oh, I thought you were the Jennings. They're late, and everyone else is here."

"Oh my," said a lady looking over his shoulder, "it's just a little girl. And look at that cute costume! Out by yourself Halloweening, dear?"

Blanche nodded and winked her nose at them. "Trick or treat?" she asked properly.

"Hey, everybody, come here!" said the man excitedly. "Look at this! She's got a neon nose!"

A dozen people got up out of their chairs and came over to crowd around the door.

"What a darling little kitty," said one lady, leaning down to pick up Brockett.

"Be careful, ma'am," said Blanche. "She doesn't like humans very much."

"Listen to that!" giggled the lady. "She said 'humans' just like she was a real little witch. Isn't she precious?"

"Aren't you out pretty late by yourself?" asked another lady, looking at her watch. "What will your mother say? It's almost midnight!"

Then Blanche remembered the Flight Meeting. It would be leaving sharp at midnight from Dead Man's Bluff!

"Excuse me, everybody," she cried out. "I've got to go right now. I'm going to be late again!"

But they made her wait while they filled her brown paper bag with chocolate mints, salted nuts, pumpkin seeds, and pretzels. Then they made her wink her nose on and off for them just one more time.

"Don't fall off your broom, little witch," said one lady fondly as Blanche ran down the front steps.

Afterwards the lady peeped out the window over the door, and gave a scream. "I'm positively sure I saw that little girl hop on her broom and fly away." The other people at the party roared

with laughter
and wouldn't be-
lieve she wasn't joking.

Aloft in the late night air, Blanche wasn't laughing. She was worried. It looked as though after all
her trouble in trying to get started on time, she was
going to be late anyhow.

As she came to Dead Man's Bluff for a landing,
she could see all of the witches in the Scurry lined
up in flight formation.

Minnie Max was pulling out her watch to show
Josephine and saying triumphantly, "You see, I
told you she'd be late again."

Blanche settled down meekly at the end of the
formation. At least they hadn't taken off yet.

Scurry No. 13 made a beautiful showing against
the moon that Halloween night. And afterwards,
they danced and sang and had refreshments up on

45

Dead Man's Bluff. Josephine ladled out the brew.

Blanche passed around the nuts, candy, pretzels, and the three jelly doughnuts carefully cut in quarters.

"Mighty good doughnuts," said the Grand Madame, looking around for more. "Where did you say you got them, Blanche?"

"Out trick or treating," said Blanche. "That's what made me late tonight. But you meet the most interesting people that way. If you ladies think you can find time for it next Halloween, I'll take you along too."

ABOUT THE AUTHOR

MARGARET JACOB EMBRY was born, reared, and educated in Salt Lake City, receiving her A.B. degree cum laude at the University of Utah. Later she lived in Los Alamos, New Mexico, with her husband and their family of four daughters and two sons. Margaret Jacob Embry died in 1975.

ABOUT THE ILLUSTRATOR

CARL ROSE studied at the Art Students League in New York, where he grew up. He has illustrated over forty books.